"I had a good da... ...idn't do anything very special. Just hung around. You know. We did go to the food store with his mom—which gives you an idea of how bored we were." He looked at the drumstick in his hand, then at Dad. "The Foleys were having steaks on the grill tonight."

"Then you should have stayed there," Dad said, laughing. "Right, Cammi?"

"Next time I will," Doug said and took a large bite of his drumstick.

I stared at my brother, almost expecting him to keel over dead. He had just told a whopper of a lie to Dad, and now he sat there eating chicken as though nothing important had happened.

"Shut your mouth, Cammi," said my little brother, Hal. "It's hanging open, and you look stupid."

The East Edge Mysteries
  • The Secret of the Burning House
  • Discovery at Denny's Deli

DISCOVERY AT
DENNY'S DELI

GAYLE ROPER

Chariot Books™
David C. Cook Publishing Co.

Published by Chariot Books,
an imprint of David C. Cook Publishing Co.
David C. Cook Publishing Co., Elgin, Illinois 60120
David C. Cook Publishing Co., Weston, Ontario
Nova Distribution, Ltd., Newton Abbot, England

DISCOVERY AT DENNY'S DELI
© 1992 by Gayle G. Roper

Cover illustration by Cindy Webber
Cover design by Helen Lannis
First printing, 1992
Printed in the United States of America
96 95 94 93 92 5 4 3 2 1

Library of Congress Cataloging-in-Publication Data
Roper, Gayle G.
Discovery at Denny's Deli/Gayle Roper
p. cm.—(An East Edge mystery)
Summary: While helping old Mrs. Bealer get ready to move from
the decaying downtown of East Edge, twelve-year-old Cammi
notices peculiar activity in the neighborhood and fears that her
older brother Doug is involved in something bad.
ISBN 1-55513-700-8
[1. Mystery and detective stories. 2. Brothers and sisters—
Fiction.] I. Title. II. Series: Roper, Gayle G.   East edge
mystery.
PZ7.R6788Di 1992
[Fic]—dc20
                                            92-5090
                                            CIP
                                            AC

*With thanks to
Becca, Crystal, and Debra
and
Carolyn and Lucy*

"You can let us off here, Dad," I said. "Mrs. Bealer's apartment is that gray one over there, the one over the tailor shop."

I pointed across the street.

Dad slowed to a stop at the corner, and Alysha and I scrambled out. It was sort of awkward, because we each had a large pile of newspapers in our arms.

"Cammi, be out here at four o'clock for Alysha's mom to pick you up," Dad said.

I nodded and slammed the car door with my hip.

"Thanks for the ride, Mr. Reston," Alysha called as Dad drove off.

While we waited for the traffic light to turn

green, Alysha tried to read her top newspaper—
a challenge because it was upside down.

"Philadelphia has a severe water shortage," she
said. "Somebody robbed a bank in Atlantic City.
The Phillies won another game. The police are
looking for some guy who escaped from jail. The
airlines are having a fare war, and now's the time
to buy tickets. There's a kid who sells so many
drugs that he's a millionaire at fifteen, and the
police can't catch him at it."

"You read all that upside down?" I was impressed.

She nodded. "But I have one question. What's a
sart?"

"A what?"

"A sart. It says here that lots of sarts were at a
big party in New York."

I looked at her paper right side up. "Star. The
word is star. Lots of stars were at the party."

Alysha laughed at her mistake and began
bouncing up and down as usual. Because she's
always moving like a miniature boxer weaving his
way around the ring, I couldn't tell if she was
nervous about today or not.

I knew that I was. I fidget when I'm nervous,
and I didn't think I'd been still since I heard about
Mrs. Bealer.

"Are you nervous?" I asked Alysha.

"About what?"

"About helping Mrs. Bealer."

"What's so hard about helping an old lady pack her things? Wrap, wrap, stuff it in a box. Wrap, wrap, stuff it in another box."

Her feet danced across the sidewalk, and her eyes sparkled. Her brown skin shone with energy. Sometimes just being with Alysha made me tired.

I squinted, not at the sun but with tension. "What if we do something wrong? What if we break something? What if we lose something? What if we don't make her happy?"

Alysha stood still long enough to stare at me. "Cammi, you worry too much!"

"But it's our first job!" I couldn't believe she wasn't feeling the pressure. "The reputation of the KCs is at stake."

"Piffle," said Alysha.

Piffle is one of her favorite words. It means the same sort of thing as fiddlesticks or who cares or so what?

"It's a family word," she told me once. "Grandpa Jackson always says it, and he says his Grandpa Jackson always said it. I'm just carrying on a family tradition."

My mother is a cop, and she's told me about

the traditions of some of the families she meets—
things like abuse and theft and drugs. Piffle
certainly is safer, even if it does sound silly.

We crossed Lincoln Highway at the light and
hurried toward Mrs. Bealer's. She had called the
Kids Care Club—less formally known as the KCs—
on Monday.

"I saw your notice on the bulletin board at
Calvary Church yesterday," she said. "I have a job
that needs to be done."

"And we have someone who can do it for you,"
said Dee Denning, our president. Like the rest of
us in the club, Dee is going into sixth grade. But
when she's on the phone, she sounds much older
and so professional. "Just tell me what you want
done and when, and we'll take care of the rest."

"I need my belongings packed for a move,"
Mrs. Bealer said. "I'm leaving my apartment in
downtown East Edge to go to Maple Shade Village.
My health isn't what it used to be, and I feel a
retirement center would be the best place for me.
They just called me about an available apartment,
so I need help as soon as possible."

"How would it be if two of our girls began Wednesday and came daily until the job is finished?"
Dee asked.

"I said Wednesday," she told Alysha and me later, "because I figured you'd need a day to learn how to pack things. Just take lots of newspapers with you for wrapping glasses and dishes and stuff. That's what the movers did when we moved here."

"Wednesday sounds wonderful," Mrs. Bealer told Dee. "I read in your notice that if I ask, you will put half the fee in the church's Help Fund."

"That's right," said Dee.

"Well, I'd like that," said Mrs. Bealer. "I'd like that a lot."

So here Alysha and I were, walking down Lincoln Highway at nine on a Wednesday morning in the beginning of August, Alysha completely calm, me fighting a dreadful case of nerves.

I looked at my reflection in the big window outside the newspaper building. I saw a girl with dirty blonde hair cut straight at her ears. I looked closer, and sure enough, I saw a pimple on my chin. Between the time I washed my face this morning and now, I'd gotten a pimple. How could that be?

At least my nerves didn't show. I took a deep breath to help me feel as cool as I looked.

As we walked past the boarded-up window of what was once a women's store, I knew deep

11

breaths weren't going to help me. Nothing was, except maybe a sudden, serious illness that would require me to go right home and stay in bed for days. Unfortunately I'm very healthy.

We stopped in front of the Army-Navy store and tried to decide which of the plaid shirts we liked best. I chose the one in tans and blues, and I could imagine my older brother, Doug, saying, "Cammi why did you pick the dull one?" Alysha, of course, liked the bright, perky red one. My nerves hated them all.

Up ahead I could see the empty J.C. Penney's store which stood across the street from the empty Sears store which stood next to what used to be Woolworth's. I always felt sort of sad looking at all the empty windows. I also missed the great grilled cheese sandwiches in Woolworth's.

"East Edge used to be the shopping center of the county," my mother told me. In fact, she told me many times. Mom has a tendency to repeat. "Then came the malls."

"And the parking meters," my father always added. He hates parking meters.

"Why does Mrs. Bealer live downtown?" I asked Alysha. "Why doesn't she get an apartment in a regular apartment complex or something?"

"This is probably cheaper," Alysha said. "And there's the drugstore." She pointed. "And the food store and the bank."

I nodded. "Convenience."

I was sweating from my load of newspapers, and I knew that when I finally set them down, I'd have the newsprint left on me in reverse print. If I got a mirror and held it to my inner arms, I could read about last week's sales.

"Help! Help! Please, no!"

The sound exploded behind us in the hot August sunshine, and we spun around to see what was wrong.

"My purse! He's got my purse!"

I barely had time to see an old woman waving her arms and looking very upset before someone bumped into me hard and sent me and my newspapers flying. I landed in a heap against a parking meter, my knees and right palm skinned and stinging, my head spinning. My papers were scattered all over the sidewalk.

I got to my feet as quickly as I could, pleased to find all my body parts still operating. Alysha was picking herself up, too. We looked at each other, nodded, and took off after the thief.

All we could see was his back. He wore jeans, a

white T-shirt, and white sneakers. He had brown hair. In short, he looked like millions of kids look from the rear—except for the patent leather purse hanging from his left hand.

"Drop that!" I yelled. "Drop it right now!"

He began to run faster. I don't think he realized anyone was after him until I shouted.

"Stop, thief!" yelled Alysha. She had two little brothers and millions of little boy cousins, and she was used to making a very big noise for someone of her small size.

But the boy didn't listen to her any better than her little brothers did. He just kept running, and so did we. He raced across the street, dodging traffic, and we followed. No one paid any attention to us except the driver of the car that swerved to miss me.

"I ought to report you to the police!" he yelled.

I waved at him because I was too out of breath to talk. I sincerely hoped he would keep his threat. We could use some help.

Suddenly the boy swerved to the left and disappeared down a narrow alley between the bank building and the old Woolworth's.

We followed, or at least we tried to. We flew around the corner of the bank smack into a

14

mother pushing a double stroller carrying twin toddlers. We fell, the babies screamed, and the mother gave us a piece of her mind. The boy with the purse got away.

Alysha and I finally untangled ourselves from
each other and the babies, and their mother
finally shut up.

"Did a kid run down here?" I asked, still
panting.

"A kid in jeans and carrying a purse?" asked
Alysha. She wasn't as out of breath as I was,
probably because of her gymnastics. Already she
was bobbing and weaving, and the mother looked
seasick from watching her.

"Yes," she said. "He came tearing around the
corner, scaring the three of us. I told him to slow
down, but he just threw something at me and kept
going. I didn't stop to find out what."

"It was a purse!" I yelled as Alysha and I went

running down the alley, looking to the right and the left.

"You shouldn't have yelled," Alysha told me. "We might have caught him!"

"Who wanted to catch him?" I said. "Not me! What would we have done with him if we'd caught him?"

"Subdue him." Alysha swung her fist through the air.

"You watch too many cop shows," I said. "He wasn't going to stand still for us, you know. He'd have beaten us up. I was just trying to make him drop the purse."

"Piffle." But she didn't look so sure anymore.

I spotted the black patent leather purse lying in a pile of leaves, beer cans, and Styrofoam cups. I grabbed it, and we ran back to where we'd left the little old lady.

But when we reached the spot where she had been, she was gone.

"Now what do we do?" Alysha asked.

I shrugged. "I guess we pick up our newspapers and go to Mrs. Bealer's. We can call the police from there."

We scurried around trying to collect our scattered papers. Somehow, no matter how hard I tried, I couldn't get mine to cooperate. They refused to fold neatly, and they insisted on taking up three times as much space as they had before.

When we finally knocked on Mrs. Bealer's door, my arms were all stiff and painful, I had ink on more than just my inner arms, and I could barely see over my load.

Alysha was having no difficulties at all.

"I'm sorry," said Mrs. Bealer when she opened her door. "I already get the paper."

"No, Mrs. Bealer," I explained. "We're not here about the papers. We're here from the Kids Care Club to help pack your things."

"My goodness," she said, peering at us in the dim hallway. "I thought you were paperboys."

Mrs. Bealer was bent over because she had a hump on her back. I'd seen other old ladies with the same problem, and I wondered how much it hurt her. Because she had very few wrinkles, her face looked much younger than her body. Which was telling us the truth about her age, I wondered, her back or her face?

She led us into her apartment. She lived on the second floor front of a big old building and had a living room, a kitchen, a bedroom, and a bathroom. The rooms were crowded with old furniture, and all the surfaces were filled with pictures and statues of pretty girls in old-fashioned dresses that looked forever like the wind was blowing them.

The thing that hit me immediately was how stuffy and hot the place was. I started to sweat in earnest. Mrs. Bealer, on the other hand, sat in her chair wearing a ratty looking, bright pink sweater over a long-sleeved dress.

She seemed fascinated with our newspapers. "Did you carry them up all those stairs?" she asked.

We nodded. I wondered if it was impolite to just dump my arm load on the floor, or whether we had to wait until she asked us to put them down. Somehow my mother never told me manners for the really tricky situations in life. Doug always says that manners just complicate life and we should do whatever we want, but I think he says it just to get Mom excited.

It didn't really matter what Mom or Doug said. I hadn't the nerve just to let go.

"Aren't they heavy?" she asked.

We nodded. I wondered if I'd ever be able to straighten my arms again. My elbows felt locked in the bent position.

"Why did you bring them?"

"To wrap your things in, so they won't break," Alysha said.

Mrs. Bealer looked confused, and I felt a moment's sudden panic.

"You do want us to pack your things, don't you? We did get the message right?"

"Yes," she said. "You belong here. I just doubt that I have enough things to use even a quarter of your papers."

"That's okay," I said, relieved we were at the right place after all. "We'll just take the leftovers home when we're finished."

Mrs. Bealer's doorbell rang, and I jumped at the loud, raspy noise. I jarred my newspapers, and they began to slide. I felt their slow, certain movement and clamped my chin on the top of the pile. Instead of stopping the avalanche, it sped it up.

Mrs. Bealer, meanwhile, was totally unaware that her living room was about to be buried.

"That bell doesn't make a very pretty sound, does it?" she asked as she walked slowly toward the door. "But at least I always hear it. Now who could it be?"

Mrs. Bealer opened her door and said, "Myra! How wonderful! And so fast!"

As she was speaking, my armful got away from

me completely. I probably shouldn't have tried to grab them as they fell. I think I just knocked them farther.

"Oh, my dear," Mrs. Bealer said as she watched her feet disappear under newspapers. "I think it would probably have been better to put them in the bedroom."

"I think so too," said Alysha as she walked into the back room and deposited her tidy pile neatly on Mrs. Bealer's bed.

I stood with my eyes closed for a second or two, waiting to hear the crash of some china lady that I had knocked off a table. My very first job for the KCs was already a total disaster, just as I had feared.

Nothing smashed itself to pieces on the floor, and I started to relax just a little. I hadn't killed any of the china ladies after all.

"My purse! Where did you get my purse?"

"What?" My eyes flew open, and I saw Mrs. Bealer's guest staring at the stolen purse, which was still hanging over my arm.

"Cammi, look!" Alysha was hopping up and down. "It's the lady we couldn't find!"

I nodded. I had recognized her, too.

"Here." I held the bag out.

"Myra Wells," said Mrs. Bealer. "Tell me what's going on."

"After you sit down, Emily," Mrs. Wells said. "You know you mustn't be on your feet too long."

I grabbed quickly at the newspapers so Mrs. Bealer could get to a chair. As I did, I noticed her feet and ankles. They were swollen terribly, and they looked very sore. She wore backless slippers and sort of slid her feet along as she walked.

"Edema," she said.

"What?"

"Edema. Swelling. That's what's wrong with my feet. I have poor circulation."

I hadn't meant to stare, but I must have. I nodded as I felt my face turn red. One of the problems with being blonde is that I blush much too easily.

"Does it hurt much?" asked Alysha.

I turned even redder. Such an impolite question!

"Sometimes more than others," said Mrs. Bealer. Alysha nodded as she skittered about the room. "My Grandma Jackson has the same problem. She usually sits with her feet up. Do you?"

"Most of the time." Mrs. Bealer hobbled to her chair and put her feet up on the big, stuffed hassock before it.

"Now, Myra," she said, "tell me what happened. Why do these girls have your purse?"

"It was stolen," Mrs. Wells said as she tried to move the air with a fold-out fan she took from her pocketbook.

Mrs. Bealer's friend was a round lady, as cushiony above the waist as below. She had on a denim skirt and a print blouse and a pair of Nikes. She had several chins that disappeared into her neck just where her blouse began.

"Stolen!" Mrs. Bealer looked at me, aghast.

"Not by us!" I said. "We found it."

Mrs. Wells came to our defense. "The girl is right, Emily. They chased the boy who grabbed it from my arm."

"We didn't catch him, though," I said. "But maybe the police will."

"And we never looked inside," Alysha said, pointing to the pocketbook. "We planned to give it to the police."

Mrs. Wells smiled. "I appreciate your honesty, but it doesn't really matter. I never put money or credit cards in it because of this very thing." She leaned close to Mrs. Bealer and us and whispered, "I keep my money in my bra."

Suddenly I had this picture of Mrs. Wells at the

checkout counter, trying to get her money, and I had to bite my tongue to keep from laughing.

"But we should still tell the police, shouldn't we?" said Alysha. "They need to know about the boy, because he might try to rob other people."

Mrs. Wells ignored Alysha and handed a plastic shopping bag to Mrs. Bealer.

"Here's your medicine and the food you needed."

Mrs. Bealer smiled and placed the bag on her lap. "Now you girls can have some lunch," she said, patting the bag.

"Alysha's right," I said. "We ought to call the police."

Mrs. Wells took the plastic bag from Mrs. Bealer's lap. "Let me take this to the kitchen," she said. "And while I'm there, I'll make us all a cup of tea." She smiled sweetly.

"That sounds lovely," said Mrs. Bealer, as she reached up and buttoned the top of her pink sweater. "I was just starting to get cold."

Cold? It must have been at least ninety degrees in that apartment. I wiped at the beads of sweat on my upper lip.

"We'll have you warm in no time, Emily. I always say nothing works better than a cup of tea to warm you from within."

Mrs. Bealer reached out and grabbed her friend's hand. "Oh, Myra, I'm going to miss you when I leave here."

Mrs. Wells smiled sadly. "And I'll miss you."

"The police," I reminded. "Do you want me to call for you?"

Mrs. Wells looked me right in the eye. "There will be no police," she said. "Do you understand?" Her voice wasn't nasty, but it was firm. "No police!"

Tea with Mrs. Bealer and Mrs. Wells was very pleasant, for the most part. Mrs. Wells had brought everything into the living room on a tray so Mrs. Bealer wouldn't have to walk to the kitchen.

We each had a flowered cup and saucer that looked like it would break if you breathed on it. Mine had pink rosebuds and violets on it, and the edge of the saucer was scalloped and painted gold. I felt like a fancy lady just holding it. When it was time to clean up, I would just call the butler and say, "Wash up everything and put it away, James. And when you're finished, pack all the china ladies into boxes."

The tea itself smelled all orangey and tasted better than I expected, though I really didn't need anything to make me feel hotter. And the muffins were great, even if they were small.

While we ate, Mrs. Bealer talked about where she was moving.

"I'll have my own one-bedroom apartment with a small kitchen area. If I get sick, there's a nurse always there and a doctor on call. I'm looking forward to it, because I've started to get nervous here."

Mrs. Wells nodded. "That's because we live alone, Emily. Living alone is not fun."

Mrs. Wells was pink from the heat. The black fan which she had taken from her purse was still fluttering, but apparently without much success.

"Oh, I don't mind being alone," Mrs. Bealer said. "I've always liked quiet and solitude. It's just I'm afraid I might fall or something, and no one would know. I don't like the idea of lying here on the floor for days. Of course," and she smiled, "the Lord would take care of me even then."

She had a very sweet smile, the kind that angels probably have.

"Well, I don't like being alone," Mrs. Wells said. She sort of clamped her mouth shut and looked stubborn, like my little brother Hal did when someone disagreed with him.

"I don't think I'd like living alone, either," said Alysha. "I've got two brothers and lots of cousins, and we all live on the same block. My favorite times are when we all get together for Sunday dinner."

"I guess it depends on whether you think being alone is lonely," said Mrs. Bealer.

"I do," said Mrs. Wells.

"Me, too," said Alysha.

"I don't," I said. "I like being alone, especially with a book."

Mrs. Bealer smiled. "My feelings exactly."

Since both women were called Mrs. but lived alone, I wanted to ask where Mr. Wells and Mr. Bealer were, but I didn't think it would be a good idea. Probably they were dead, and I'd just make the ladies sad. Instead I looked hopefully at the now empty muffin dish, but none had magically appeared since my last glance.

"Do you have much trouble with people like that kid today?" asked Alysha. Even as she sat, she was moving, her legs swinging back and forth like the pendulum on my grandmother's big clock. "Robbers don't come up to your apartments or anything, do they?"

"None has ever come to mine," answered Mrs. Wells.

"Nor mine," said Mrs. Bealer. "Of course, I keep my door locked all the time."

Mrs. Wells nodded. "Double locked."

"Windows, too," said Mrs. Bealer. "All the time."

That explained the stuffiness.

"Have you ever had your purse stolen before?" I asked.

Mrs. Wells shook her head no and took another drink of tea. I noticed her purse was leaning against the leg of her chair so she'd know exactly where it was.

"I've heard of it happening to other older women," Mrs. Bealer said. "Mrs. Patton, Myra. Remember? They sneaked up behind her and grabbed her purse and ran. They knew she couldn't chase them. And she didn't have these two wonderful girls around."

I smiled and said, "I know he didn't get your money, Mrs. Wells, but did he get anything else? Credit cards? License? We can still call the police."

Mrs. Wells smiled slightly. "I only carry things like Kleenex and Tums and my fan in my purse. If anyone takes it, it doesn't matter."

"Sure, it does," I said.

"No, it doesn't," she said tightly. "The things have no value."

"But it's wrong."

Mrs. Wells suddenly became angry. Her eyes shot sparks as she glared at me. "We will not talk about my purse anymore. Do you understand? Nor will we discuss calling the police. The issue is dead!"

There was a short, awkward silence which I spent looking at the floor. I guess because of my mom, I always think the police are the best and only answer to a problem like theft. It made no sense to me not to report it. But I was very embarrassed about ruining the tea party.

Finally Mrs. Bealer said briskly, "Well, Myra, this tea has certainly hit the spot. I'm not chilly anymore."

"Wonderful!" said Mrs. Wells, all smiles and charm again. "I told you it would work."

"Let me help carry the cups back to the kitchen," Alysha said as she took mine from my hand, and we all became very busy clearing up the tea things. My imaginary James didn't put in an appearance.

Then Alysha and I followed Mrs. Bealer into her bedroom, where she gave us instructions.

"Now, girls, you will have to make several trips to the grocery store down the street and collect the boxes they have been saving for me. Just knock on the office door and tell them I sent you.

31

"Of course, the books won't have to be wrapped in your newspaper," she said, smiling. "Just dust them well before you pack them."

We looked at her bookshelves, which covered one entire wall from floor to ceiling.

"How many books do you think there are?" Alysha asked after Mrs. Bealer hobbled back to her chair.

"I don't know, but they'll take a lot of boxes. And how will we ever reach the top shelves?"

We stared up until our necks got kinks, then looked at each other and said together, "Shannon!"

Shannon Symmonds belongs to the KCs and is very tall.

"We'll ask her to come with us tomorrow," I said.

Alysha nodded, and we headed out the door for our first load of boxes.

Back at the apartment, we got down to business. After a while Alysha broke the silence.

"Mrs. Wells certainly got mad at you."

"I know, but why? The cops would only try to help."

"Not everyone's as comfortable around police as you are, Cammi." She put one hand over her head and gave a mighty jump, trying to see how high she could reach. "Beat that jump, if you can," she said with satisfaction.

Instead I pulled down a book that had a brown leather cover and gold lettering. I held it to my nose and enjoyed the musty, dusty smell. Libraries smell like that sometimes. I think it's the smell of knowledge.

We were returning from our last trip to the grocery store for boxes when I glanced across the street and almost dropped my arm load.

"Alysha! Look! It's him!"

The kid who had taken Mrs. Wells's purse was walking down the street as big as life. He was with two other guys, and he had a Popsicle in his hand which he was trying to eat it before it melted. He kept bending over and slurping at the bottom.

One of the guys with him was very tough looking. He was both tall and heavy, and I could see a tattoo on his arm because he had his T-shirt sleeves rolled all the way up to his shoulders. There was a package of cigarettes tucked into the rolled sleeve cuff, and he wore sunglasses that were mirrors on the outside, the ones where you saw yourself whenever you looked at the wearer.

The third boy was smaller, but the big guy partially blocked him from my view. All I could see was a pair of Reeboks and socks shuffling along with the others.

"Are you sure he's the thief?" Alysha asked, squinting across the street. "Who's he with? What should we do?"

"I don't know who he's with, and I don't know if there's anything we can do if Mrs. Wells won't call the police."

"How can you be so sure it's him?" Alysha's voice was uncertain. "We only saw his back."

"Of course it's him," I said. "I recognize him."

I stared at the boy. He looked about sixteen, with the skinny body of someone who eats all the time and never gains any weight. He had big feet he hadn't grown into yet, and they looked even bigger in his white high tops. When he had knocked us down, he had looked pretty big to me, but now, walking next to a truly big kid, he looked much less scary.

His Popsicle suddenly broke apart, and he stopped to catch the pieces and eat them before they melted into a purple puddle in his hands.

His two friends walked a couple of steps before they stopped and turned. The big one no longer blocked my view of the third one, and I found myself staring across the street at my older brother Doug.

I opened my mouth but nothing came out. I wasn't sure whether I was going to call Doug's name or gag good and loud at the company he was keeping.

If Dad ever saw him hanging around with a guy with a tattoo and cigarettes, to say nothing of a guy who was a thief, Doug wouldn't get out of the house for months.

Dad is a high school principal, and he has very strict rules for us. He always says he's seen too many kids get in trouble because their parents don't care, and, by gum, he's not falling into that trap.

I don't mind his rules too much, and neither does Hal, but at fourteen, Doug is complaining more and more.

"My father's a principal and my mother's a cop!" he said one evening at the beginning of the summer as we sat in the backyard eating popcorn and drinking iced tea. "I haven't got a chance. If people don't hate me for one parent, they hate me for the other."

"Well, I'm sorry about that," said Dad, "but neither of us is quitting work. You know as well as I, Doug, that plenty of people are impressed by what Mom and I do. What would you prefer? That Mom was a bag lady and I was a junkie?"

"Some days that sounds good," Doug said.

"There's one advantage principals and cops have over bag ladies and junkies," Mom said. "We tend to bring money home regularly to feed our kids."

"I think it's neat you're a principal," I said to Dad, "and that you're a cop."

Mom smiled and Dad patted my knee, then took some more popcorn.

"You know," Doug said, "if you were in another school district or Mom was a cop in another town, it wouldn't be quite so bad. As it is, it couldn't be worse."

Dad smiled at Doug's overreaction, but Doug didn't. He was serious. I could tell because he wasn't eating. Ordinarily Doug eats anything he can get his hands on, even though it doesn't seem to be doing him much good. He hasn't grown very tall. ("Yet," Mom always says. "He hasn't grown very tall *yet*.")

"There's one more thing we have to talk about," Doug said that night. "On days when you and Mom are both gone, I can just stay home, right? I don't have to go to Tim's unless I feel like it."

For years, when Mom has worked day shift, Doug has gone to our neighbor's house. When she works evenings or nights, there's no problem because Dad is usually home. If he has a meeting, a baby-sitter comes. Now Doug wanted independence.

Dad thought before he answered. He's told us a hundred times that junior high is a tricky time. Letting Doug stay home alone would be a big change of opinion.

"Dad, for Pete's sake!" Doug said, throwing his hands up in the air. He forgot he was holding a cup of popcorn, and the kernels flew. "All my friends stay home alone all the time. I'm the only one who doesn't, and I feel like a prize fool. Don't you trust me?"

"Compromise," said Dad. "Two days a week

you can stay here. The other three, I'd like you to go to Tim's."

Doug wasn't very happy.

"Remember—no one inside without Mom or me being here," Dad added.

Doug stalked into the house shaking his head and muttering to himself about the general unfairness of parents.

Doug is a special person to me. Sometimes he gets grumpy, the way he did when Dad said no to his staying alone all the time, but usually he's fine. He's always been extra nice to me, his little sister, for as long as I can remember. And I remember all the way back to the day he taught me to blow my nose.

"You can't remember that," Doug said to me once. "You were only three."

"I remember," I said. "I had a bad cold, and I kept sniffing and swallowing and feeling sick to my stomach. Mom kept telling me to blow, and I kept inhaling. You asked me if I could blow out the candles on a birthday cake, and I told you that of course I could. 'Show me,' you said. 'Make believe there's a cake right here.' And you held out your hands. I blew. You had me inhaling and blowing and inhaling and blowing. 'Now blow them out with your nose,' you said, and I did.

38

I used up a whole box of tissues practicing my new trick, and Mom didn't even care."

Then Doug was seven; now he was fourteen and moody and a teenager. But he had two free days.

"It's better than nothing," I told him later that night.

"I guess," he said.

Then came the fire at our house and the temporary move to Green Springs while the house was being repaired. And now I had the answer to why I was so sure that the guy with Doug was the one who had snatched Mrs. Wells's purse. I had seen him before at our apartment complex. I'd never talked to him or anything, just seen him like you see someone you don't really know. They're there, but they're not.

I didn't know anything about the guy, except that he was a thief and he could run fast. And my brother was hanging around with him, laughing with him as he slurped the last of his Popsicle and rubbed his sticky hands on his jeans.

I turned to Alysha, but she was already up the steps to Mrs. Bealer's.

"Get the door for me, Cammi, and I'll get the door for you."

39

Obviously she hadn't seen Doug.

I turned back, and just that quickly Doug was gone. So was the thief. All I saw was the door of Denny's Deli sliding shut behind the big guy.

My stomach was churning. Not only was Doug hanging around with scary guys, but Denny's Deli had a really bad reputation in East Edge. There were whispers of drugs and underage drinking and stuff. Mom said the cops patrolled near it frequently to keep order.

So what was my brother-the-good-guy doing in a place like that . . . and what would Dad do when he found out?

While I held the door for Alysha, I thought about Doug. He had never been in trouble before, and he probably had a good reason for being in Denny's, though I couldn't for the life of me think of one. Still, that didn't mean there wasn't one. Did it?

Alysha and I banged our way up the stairs. If those boxes had had hard corners, the walls would have looked like Swiss cheese.

Poor Mrs. Bealer. Her living room was so full of boxes she could hardly see the TV, and we could hardly get to the bedroom.

"Be sure to leave me a path to my bed and a

path to the bathroom," Mrs. Bealer said. "Once those boxes are filled with books, I'll never be able to move them. Help yourselves to Cokes from the refrigerator, girls, before you go back to packing."

We drank thirstily and got back to work. I forgot about Doug as I enjoyed the books.

"Isn't this beautiful?" I asked Alysha. I held up a volume of William Shakespeare, a famous writer who lived long ago. The book was tan leather with gold leaf on the edges of the pages, just like my mom's Bible. I opened the front and found some faded, spiky handwriting that read, "To Eleanor, my own true love, from Charles, 1898."

"1898! This book is almost a hundred years old!" I rubbed my hand gently over the lettering, then set it down and looked in the rest of the Shakespeare books. They all had the same inscription.

"Mrs. Bealer." I went to the door and held out the book. "Who were Eleanor and Charles?"

"My mother and father," she said with her special smile. "He gave them to her as a wedding gift. He was an English professor, and he loved good books. I remember him reading aloud from them. I was very small and didn't understand much, but I remember how beautiful the words sounded when he said them."

"Didn't he read when you got older?"

"Probably. I was just too busy to listen. I was what used to be called a tomboy."

I stared at Mrs. Bealer with her white hair and pink sweater and swollen feet, trying to imagine her as a tomboy. It was very hard, and I have a good imagination.

I felt a poke in my ribs.

"The job, Cammi," Alysha whispered in my ear. "I really don't want to pack all these books by myself."

"Don't you want to read all of them?" I asked as I laid the Shakespeare gently in a box. "Don't you want to know whose they were, where they came from, and how old they are?"

Alysha looked at me strangely and shook her head. "I don't know about you, Cammi. Sometimes I think you're going to end up a librarian."

"Would that be so awful?" I asked.

Alysha snorted. She grabbed books and stuffed them in boxes so fast my eyes could hardly follow her. Obviously any job where you sat still seemed ridiculous to her.

"How do you like Green Springs?" she asked. "Is it still terrible?"

"It's not Green Springs that's terrible," I said.

"It's a nice enough place. It's being away from home that's terrible."

I thought about Hampton Street. I missed the maple trees that lined the sidewalk, the woods behind our house, and our large yard where you could run without looking out for cars or baby strollers or bicycles. I thought of my rose bedroom and of my doll collection, now living at Dee's house. I missed it all a lot.

"And I miss Beast. He can't live at Green Springs because dogs aren't allowed. I know Dee's taking good care of him, but I want to be the one taking care of him."

Beast is our Newfoundland, a huge, black, shaggy monster who is the best face washer I've ever met. Any time I feel sad, all I have to do is hug him and I feel better.

"And we haven't found Bugs yet."

Bugs is my big, gray cat who disappeared the night of the fire.

"You still cry over him every night?" Alysha asked.

"Only every other night," I said. I knew she thought I was crazy to care so much. "The worst thing, though—the very worst—is that at Green Springs we have a two-bedroom apartment, and I have to share a room with my little brother who talks in his sleep and is the sloppiest kid who ever lived. I can never find what I want because either he's lost it for me or it's back at the house covered with soot."

I hugged the dictionary I was holding, not because I loved it but because all of a sudden I felt really insecure. A new job. An older lady who got mad at me. A brother who was behaving oddly. An apartment I disliked. A dog and a cat I missed. I felt about three years old and all I wanted to do was yell at the top of my lungs, "I wanna go home!"

I stood in the door to my bedroom and stared. How did Hal do it? There wasn't a free piece of space anywhere!

I went to my bed and grabbed everything lying on it, then turned and dumped it all on Hal's bed. My guess was he wouldn't even notice.

I flopped on my bed—my temporary bed, I reminded myself—and stared at the ceiling. I was tired from working.

I grinned. I sounded like my parents.

"Turn the TV down, will you, please?" Dad always said. "I'm tired and I'd like a little peace."

"Kids," Mom would yell, "turn that music down or put on earphones! I'm tired and I can't take that volume! And I want you to know that if your earphones make you deaf, I'm not paying for your hearing aids."

Hal came flying into the room, lips blue, skin pruney, hair sticking out all over, bathing suit dripping.

"Out, Cammi," he said. "I need to get dressed."

"You get out," I said conversationally. "Take your stuff to the bathroom and change. That way you can hang your suit in the tub instead of leaving it to rot on the floor like usual."

"Okay," he said, surprising me. He grabbed an armful of clothes and fled. He must have been very cold if he didn't take time to argue with me.

I rolled off the bed and went to the phone.

"Shannon?" I said. "Can you come with Alysha and me to the job tomorrow? Mrs. Bealer has high shelves, and they're all full of books."

"Hey, Mom," yelled Shannon without moving the phone, "can I go with Cammi and Alysha tomorrow?"

I jerked the phone from my ear and listened to Shannon's voice rattle around in my head. It wasn't earphones that would make me deaf. If Shannon just opened her window and talked, all East Edge would hear. Having her yell when she's two inches from the phone is like someone blowing a trumpet in your ear!

"What's Mrs. Bealer going to do with all her books?" Shannon asked.

Pleased that I could still hear, I said, "I have no idea. Take them to her new home, I guess."

"Really? Grandmom Symmonds lives at the same place Mrs. Bealer's going, and she doesn't have room for a lot of books in her place. I was just there last Sunday, and it isn't very large."

"Maybe Mrs. Bealer's room is bigger. Or maybe she's giving them to the library. Who knows?"

But I wondered. An old book collection would be nice to keep my dolls company.

I'd just finished making arrangements to pick Shannon up the next day when Dad called.

"Dinner! Come and get it."

I went to the table and found a large tub of Kentucky Fried Chicken sitting there. Mom must be working the three to eleven shift.

I didn't mind when she worked day shift, and I really didn't mind nights (after all, I was asleep), but I hated three to eleven.

I sat down and waited with Dad for Hal and Doug who, as usual, took their sweet time. We ate at six o'clock every night, come rain or shine, but for some reason the boys were often late. Then again, maybe they just knew which nights Dad was the dinner person.

Usually when Mom worked evenings, she left us dinner in the oven or refrigerator. She liked to cook, and she left us gooey casseroles full of cheese and hamburger or stews with wonderful gravies or her very best, spaghetti. But when things were really busy or crazy (like with trying to get the house repaired) and she couldn't get to the food, Dad was responsible for feeding us.

KFC and pizza were his favorites. Once we had pizza four nights in a row. I was always glad when Mom's shift changed to eleven to seven. She might have been sleepy all the time, but we ate decently.

"Thanks for this food, Lord," Dad prayed. "We appreciate Your kindness to us. And protect Mom tonight at work."

For a while the only sound was chewing. Then Dad said his usual, "I love this coleslaw!"

He always said it, and he always said it with an exclamation point. If KFC ever changes its coleslaw recipe, Dad will undoubtedly sue.

"So, how did today go, Hal?" Dad asked.

"Great," Hal said. "Mom was at our house on Hampton Street with the painters, so the Denning twins and I played in the woods behind the house.

We're building a fort. Then Mom drove us over here about two and dropped us at the apartment pool. Mrs. Denning came, too, and watched us until they had to go home. Then I came home, too, and here I am."

Dad nodded. He liked good, solid, no excitement days.

"Oh," Hal said, like he just remembered. "Cammi, we may have seen Bugs."

"What?" My heart began to pound. "Where?"

"When Mike, Phil, and I walked into the woods, this animal streaked off into the underbrush. It was big and gray like Bugs, but I didn't see it well enough to be certain. It could have been a big squirrel or something."

"Oh, Hal!" I couldn't stop smiling. It was the first word about Bugs since the fire.

"We left some food and water at the fort," Hal said. "Just in case."

"What a brother!" I tried to hug him, and he did his best to hold me off, but I could tell by his smile that he was happy to make me happy.

"Good thinking, Hal," said Dad. "Good thinking." Maybe it was part of being a principal, but he loved it when we showed signs of what he called "mature and independent thought."

"And now, Doug, how was your day?"

I was so excited at the idea of Bugs being seen that I almost missed Doug's answer. Then I wished I had.

"I had a good day, too, Dad," Doug said. "Tim and I didn't do anything very special. Just hung around. You know. We did go to the food store with his mom—which gives you an idea of how bored we were." He looked at the drumstick in his hand, then at Dad. "The Foleys were having steaks on the grill tonight."

"Then you should have stayed there," Dad said, laughing. "Right, Cammi?"

"Next time I will," Doug said and took a large bite of his drumstick.

I stared at my brother, almost expecting him to keel over dead. He had lied to Dad, and now he was eating chicken like nothing important had happened.

"Shut your mouth, Cammi," Hal said. "It's hanging open, and you look stupid."

"Shut yours," I said, but halfheartedly. "You sound stupid."

"That's enough," said Dad. "Now, tell us about your day, Cammi."

I found it hard to concentrate on the story of

Mrs. Wells and her purse with Doug sitting there like nothing was wrong, like he hadn't spent the day with the very thief I was telling about. I felt like I ought to check his breath to see whether he'd been smoking or his chest to make certain he hadn't gotten a tattoo or something.

"And she wouldn't let you call the police?" Dad said when I finished my story.

I shook my head. "She got really mad at me about it. But I know who the kid is. I mean, I don't know his name, but I've seen him around."

I watched Doug as I spoke to see how he'd react. He didn't.

"I think the kid lives here at Green Springs," I said.

Did Doug hesitate there for a minute?

"Here?" Hal said excitedly.

"Are you certain?" Dad asked. "You don't want to misidentify someone, you know."

"I know who it is," I said. "I'm absolutely certain."

"What's he look like?" Dad asked.

I thought for a minute and realized there was nothing special about him. He was just a kid like millions of other kids. No limps or hair to his waist, no eyes in the back of his head or third arm.

51

"He looks like any other kid," I said. "Jeans, high tops, dark hair. He's skinny and runs pretty well, even with a purse in his hand."

"But you don't know his name?"

I shook my head, not certain what to say next. Should I say that while I might not know who he was, Doug certainly did? After all, they had spent the day together and my dear older brother had just told one of the biggest lies I'd ever heard when he claimed to be with Tim.

"I've seen him hanging around the apartment pool," I said, "but he never goes in the water."

"Maybe he can't swim," Hal said. "He's scared of the water."

"Well, anyone who would rob an old lady can't be very courageous," Dad said. "You'll have to point him out to me, Cammi. I might know him from school."

The phone rang, and Hal jumped to answer it. While we waited to see who it was for, I was aware of Doug watching me carefully.

He's wondering what I know, I thought. *He's trying to decide whether I'm talking about his friend or not. He hasn't a clue that I know anything bad about him. After all, he didn't try to snatch a purse. At least not today. But tomorrow?*

Suddenly my chicken began flying around in my stomach, and I thought I might be sick right there at the table. I knew I had to tell on Doug. I had to. Didn't I?

But I'll get him into big trouble.

He deserved to be in trouble. He'd lied. And how many other days had he lied? For all I knew, he hadn't been to Tim's house since we came to Green Springs.

But if I tell, he'll hate me forever! I'll be a rat and a stool pigeon, a squealer and a tattletale.

But if I didn't, he could end up in jail.

That old jump rope chant kept pounding through my head:

Tattletale, ginger ale,
Stick your head in the garbage pail.
Turn it in, turn it out,
Turn it into sauerkraut.

"Dad," I began, but Hal cut me off as he hung up the phone.

"Cammi, the girls are going to Brooke's to swim. Your ride will be here in about ten minutes."

I groaned and made a face. I always make faces when anyone mentions Brooke Picardy.

Brooke is very pretty, very rich, and very smart, and she doesn't mind telling you so. She also doesn't mind telling you that you aren't. And she *always* knows best.

"Cammi," she'll say, "you didn't actually volunteer to help with the little kids, did you?" Laugh, laugh. "How funny you are."

"Cammi, you don't seriously plan to wear that to school, do you?" Laugh, laugh. "How embarrassing for you."

"Cammi, you only got a B on that test?" Laugh, laugh. "How unintelligent of you."

She and I are in the same grade in school and the same Sunday school class at church. As if all that forced time together isn't bad enough, her parents—who are very nice people—happen to be my parents' best friends, so I get to see even more of her, hooray, hooray.

What I can't figure out is how she knows everything. How does she know what's the latest style? How does she know what color looks nicest? How does she know the best haircut—and how to keep it looking nice? How does she know who the hottest singers are? How does she know what the boys like? It's all a mystery to me.

"I don't want to go to her house," I said.

"Now, Cammi," said Dad. I think he knows Brooke is a terrible person, but he doesn't want to admit it. He wants me to like her because he and Mom like Mr. and Mrs. Picardy. So he keeps trying to soothe me.

"Don't now-Cammi me," I said. "None of you guys has to go everywhere with her like I do. Not you, Doug, not you, Hal, and certainly not you, Dad."

"Thank goodness!" said Doug with great feeling.

I grinned. Brooke thought Doug was "the cutest thing in this world," and he ran like crazy whenever she came into view. I often thought that the one thing she didn't know about life was how to impress my brother.

"I think you should go, Cammi," said Dad. "You're a good influence on her."

I stared at Dad. "Are you kidding? She never listens to a thing I say. She's too busy criticizing me. She's always telling me how awful I look or how dumb I am or something. And you know what scares me? What if she's right?"

I felt gloomy, like I was slipping into a black hole. Only Brooke could make me feel this bad.

"Don't pay any attention to her, kid," said Doug. "You're so much smarter and prettier and nicer than she is, it's not even close. You just remember that." And he smiled warmly across the table.

I stared back, stunned. Doug had never said I was pretty before. How could I rat on him now?

"Honey," said Dad, "you certainly don't have to go to Brooke's if you don't want to. I will ask you, however, to call and say you're not coming."

"Who was going to pick me up?" I asked Hal as I started for the phone.

"Gail," he said.

Suddenly the whole evening looked different. If Gail was going, it couldn't be too bad. Her presence always made Brooke watch her mouth.

Gail Macklinburg was our Sunday school teacher, and we all loved her. She was wonderful, and for some reason, no guy had been smart enough to figure it out yet. I personally hoped none did until I was out of her class. Not that I wanted her to be single forever if she had other ideas, but I didn't want some guy poking his nose in, either.

But the best thing about seeing Gail tonight was that I could ask her advice about Doug. I took a deep breath. I felt better already.

Brooke's mother came from a rich, rich family, and the Picardys' house showed it. It was gorgeous, big, built of tan bricks, and it looked so wonderful that I was always surprised people actually lived in it.

The outside was perfect, with all the plants growing just the right height and not a weed daring to show its face. There wasn't a single wilted flower in the gardens, and the lawn was bright green, even in the middle of a Pennsylvania August. The pool was big and blue, and a spa bubbled at one end.

The inside of the house was like a magazine. There were always fresh flowers all over the place, and everything was neat, neat, neat (as in orderly, not nifty). I had never seen the place without parallel sweeper marks in the rugs. Natalie, the maid, must spend hours just making those lines all go the same direction.

In fact, the rugs were so deep that once when

we were there when Hal was little, he couldn't walk on them without falling. At least he didn't hurt himself. In fact, he sort of bounced.

"Well, Cammi, our little refugee," Brooke greeted me. "How are you tonight?"

Somehow her tone of voice made me feel like the towel in my hand was actually a packet in which I had rolled all my worldly goods, and I was sentenced to wander forever in search of some spot to lay my weary and homeless head.

"She's amazing, isn't she?" Dee Denning said as we stood in the shallow end of the pool. "In one simple sentence she can reduce any of us to idiots."

"Not you," I said. "You give her a run for her money."

"I try," Dee said.

I'm not certain what pastors' daughters are supposed to be like, and maybe sometimes Dee isn't the perfect one, but I like her a lot. I've been around when she and Brooke have bumped heads, and Brooke doesn't automatically win.

With me, however, Brooke doesn't just win. She triumphs.

In spite of Brooke, it was nice to swim after the stuffy day at Mrs. Bealer's. Dee's a water baby and an organizer, so soon she had us trying water ballets and swimming across the pool underwater and stuff I loved it.

Gail swam the farthest underwater, but Dee said it was because she was the tallest. Shannon called for a measuring, because she thought *she* was tallest. And she was.

"Okay," said Dee, "Gail won because she's the oldest."

No one could disagree with that. She is, after all, twenty-eight.

Through all this fun, Brooke sat on the edge of the pool looking bored. She had on her black, I-want-to-look-like-an-adult swimsuit, and she did look pretty mature—if you ignored the fact that she had no chest.

Of course, I couldn't criticize. Neither do I. But at least I know it and act like a kid to match my looks.

At one point Alysha and I met at the edge of the pool. She was getting ready to dive, and the setting sun shone on her bent head. I loved the way the water sort of beaded on her hair instead of making it all stringy like mine.

"I wonder if Mrs. Bealer would let us use an electric fan tomorrow while we're working," I said.

"Let's just take one," she called as she flew over my head. If Alysha's active on land, water sends her into overdrive. She raced from my side of the pool to the other, then yelled, "Do you have a fan? We don't, because we have central air conditioning."

"I don't know," I yelled back, cupping my hands around my mouth to make the sound project better. "We used to have one, but I have no idea if we do anymore. It could have been ruined by the fire, or it could be at the house, or it could be at the apartment. I'll check."

"Always the lady, aren't you, Cammi?" Brooke smiled sweetly from poolside as she twisted the knife in my back. "So soft-spoken and genteel."

Now I was not only a refugee, I was also a loudmouth. If I had any masking tape, there would be no doubt what Brooke thought I should tape shut.

I looked around for Gail. She'd save me from any more of Brooke's hospitality. Besides, I needed to talk with her about Doug.

"This was a nice idea, Gail," I said as I joined her. She was leaning against the side of the pool kicking her legs gently. "Swimming feels so relaxing after a hot day working."

She grinned. Her long, dark hair was pulled back into a ponytail, and her bangs were plastered to her forehead. Somehow, she looked beautiful. "How's your job going?"

"Mrs. Bealer's a nice old lady, and I love all her books. If she didn't insist on keeping all the doors and windows shut, it'd probably be a little better, but I'll survive."

"Take a fan," Gail said. "And just open the window in whatever room you're working."

"Would that be okay? I don't want to upset her."

"She won't mind," Gail said. "She just doesn't realize how hot it is in there. I was going to help her move Saturday, and believe me, I planned to open windows. But her family's coming to help, so she doesn't need me. I'm glad, because it turns out I can't be there after all. I'm leaving Friday night for the rest of the summer."

"Where are you going?" I asked.

"To Camp Harmony Hill. I'm going to be the camp nurse for the last three weeks of the season. The regular nurse has to leave because her mother is very ill. I'm the fill-in."

"Poison ivy," I said. "That's what you'll have to treat. There's tons of poison ivy at Harmony Hill."

She made a face. "Not very exciting. But it's better than broken bones and painful diseases, at least for the campers."

"My parents have signed me up for a week at Harmony Hill near the end of August," said Dee as she joined us. "Is it as nice as I hear?"

As president of the KCs, Dee was such a part of our group that it was hard to remember she had only moved here this summer and didn't know about lots of local things yet.

I nodded. "It's beautiful, with lots of woods and a huge pool and a stream for boating and horses and archery and all kinds of things. I love it."

"Have you been there often?" Dee asked.

"Every year since first grade. If I could, I'd stay all summer, but my mom's convinced I'd miss them too much." I grinned. "Don't tell them, but I don't think I would. I can't wait until I'm old enough to be a CIT."

"What's a CIT?" Dee asked.

"A counselor-in-training. Then after a couple of summers doing that, you get old enough to be a junior counselor and then, finally, a counselor."

Dee looked pleased. "Everybody has told me the same good things about this place, so it must be great. We'll have KCs Week at Harmony Hill.

It'll be such fun, especially with you there, too, Gail!"

I felt my heart turn to stone and sink to my toes. So everybody was going, just like usual. For the last few weeks, I'd been hoping that if I didn't talk about Harmony Hill, everyone would forget how great it was, and nobody would remember to sign up.

My plan had failed.

"I'm not going this summer," I said.

Dee and Gail both looked surprised.

"But it's your favorite place and you always go," said Gail.

"I don't want to go this year," I lied. Then I dived and swam to the deep end before anyone could say anything more.

The truth was, I wanted to go to Harmony Hill so much I could taste it. But with the fire and all, there wasn't enough money for camp this summer. We had insurance to take care of a lot of the damage, and people had given us gifts and money and stuff. But the truth was, all the repairs were costing more than we had.

"Everything's lost," I'd overheard Mom say to Dad one day shortly after the fire. "Even Harmony Hill's gone up in smoke."

Now I bit my lip and blinked away tears as I "hid" under the diving board. I didn't want anybody to see me crying, especially not Brooke. She'd never let me live it down, and it hurt bad enough without any help from her.

"Gail, can I ask you a quick question?"

We were seated in the front of the van on the way home.

I glanced over my shoulder and saw Shannon and Bethany Stoller laughing about something. Alysha was bouncing up and down and Dee, who was sharing her seat, looked sick to her stomach. A couple of other girls in our Sunday school class were in the far back seat with their heads together.

They all looked too involved to pay any attention to me, which was good. I didn't want them to hear what I had to say

I glanced back again and took a deep breath.

"What if someone is doing something wrong?" I asked Gail. "Well, he hasn't done anything really wrong yet. But he's hanging around with people he shouldn't, and one of those people did something really wrong. I know because I saw him do it. My person hasn't done anything like that. At least I don't think so. I mean, he's lied. I know he's lied. I heard him. I know that was wrong, but I'm afraid he's going to do something really wrong and get into lots of trouble. But he hasn't yet, I don't think."

I was babbling. Gail probably had no idea what I trying to say. I felt a heavy weight on my chest, like I was lying on my back and all the KCs were standing on top of me. Part of the weight was fear for Doug, part was shame for myself. I can be such a dummy.

"Anyway," I said as we pulled up in front of our apartment, "should I tell on him? I mean, he hasn't done anything yet."

The back of the van was quieting down. They were all listening, I knew. They were all waiting to see why I wasn't getting out of the van.

Gail looked at me and smiled.

"I have one general rule," she said. "My mom gave it to me years ago, and it's still a good rule."

Hurry, I thought. *They're all listening.*

"If someone does something that could hurt

68

himself or someone else, you tell. Or if they're doing something that the Bible says specifically they shouldn't, like lying. If they're doing something dumb or silly or something you don't like—but it's not dangerous or sinful, just dumb—then you ignore it."

I stared at Gail. What a great rule!

"Who do you tell?" I asked.

"Whoever's in charge," she said.

"Thank you!" I said, searching for the door handle. Why don't cars put all their handles in the same place? I wanted to get out before someone in the back of the van asked me what I was talking about. "Thank you!"

"You could always talk to the person you're worried about," Gail said. "Ask him what's going on, and tell him you know what he's doing. Maybe he'll shape up on his own."

I stared at her. Talk to Doug before I told Mom and Dad? I'd never thought of that.

Suddenly the back seat exploded in laughter. I looked back and saw all the girls grouped around Shannon. They'd been listening to her, not to me, and they probably didn't even know we had been sitting in the parking lot at Green Springs. I was safe!

The van door finally popped open, and I almost fell out.

"Have a good time at Harmony Hill, Gail," I said and slipped to the ground. "Bye!" I waved to the girls, delighted that no one even noticed I was leaving. I slammed the door and raced up the walk.

Talk with Doug. Ask him what was going on before I told Mom and Dad. Then, if he didn't tell the truth and if he didn't stop hanging around with that kid, I would tell.

What he was doing was both dangerous and wrong. He was hanging around with a guy who was a thief, and he was lying.

I shut the front door behind me and just stood in the hall, thinking. For some reason, the idea of talking to Doug made my insides feel like I had a bad stomach virus.

Why didn't I want to talk to him? I'd never felt that way before.

I finally realized it was because he'd lied. If he'd lied to Dad, why wouldn't he lie to me? And I didn't want to be lied to. Not by my brother.

Doug is smart and handsome and clever and my protector whenever anyone tries to pick on me.

Mom tells a story about when I was two and Doug almost five. A big strange dog ran into our yard and jumped into my playpen. The dog began to kiss me, and I began to scream.

Doug climbed into the playpen with me and this huge dog and tried to get him to jump out. By the time Mom got to us, I was standing in one corner shrieking and Doug was standing in another with his arms under the dog's stomach, trying to move him. Since Doug and the dog were the same height, Doug wasn't having much success. The dog was standing in the center of the playpen, smiling and drooling, having a wonderful time.

I don't remember that time at all, but I do remember when I was four and we were at a fair. Dad had bought me a snow cone.

"Stand right here, Cammi," he had said. "Don't move. The rest of us are getting ours and I have to pay for them."

I stood rooted to my spot eating my cone when suddenly an older boy appeared at my side.

"Gimme that, kid," he said and reached for my snow cone.

I was too surprised and scared to make any noise at all.

Suddenly seven-year-old Doug ran to my side and dumped his entire grape snow cone down the guy's front.

The kid was furious because of the stain and because it was so cold.

"You owe me a new shirt!" he yelled. "Look what you did! My mom's going to kill me! This was brand new!"

Dad had come running at the commotion and scolded Doug because he was all thumbs. Doug had stood there and listened to Dad, waiting to explain.

"But, Daddy—" he started.

"No excuses, Douglas," Dad said. "You were careless."

"No, Daddy," I said when Dad reached into his pocket for his wallet to pay the kid for a new shirt. "Dougie saved me and my snow cone."

The kid heard me, saw my father's face, and took off while he could still run.

Doug got anything he wanted for the rest of that day.

Once when I was in third grade and Doug was in sixth, he even got beat up for me.

It was a snowy winter day, and the hill on 11th Avenue was roped off for us kids. Doug was allowed to go sledding if he took me along. Since the hill was only two blocks from our house, it wasn't too bad for him, especially since I didn't have a sled.

I spent most of my time sitting happily on the curb watching, but one time Doug let me use his sled. I lay on my tummy, and he gave me a push. I was scared, but doing okay, when some kid decided to ram into me and push me into the parked cars at the curb.

The next thing I knew, Doug was on the kid's back, punching at him. The kid yelped, and all his friends came to his aid.

Poor Doug. He got a bloody nose and a black eye from an icy snowball. I didn't get hurt.

And at supper he'd said I was smarter and prettier than Brooke.

Tattletale, ginger ale,
Stick your head in the garbage pail.
Turn it in, turn it out,
Turn it into sauerkraut.

Yes, I would talk to him before I said anything to Mom and Dad. He deserved it. He had earned a chance to make things all right just by being Doug all these years.

The phone rang, and I picked it up. Doug's friend Tim was on the other end.

I slumped on the sofa and watched Doug talk to Tim. I could tell from the conversation that Tim wanted him to go to the shore for the day tomorrow. And Doug obviously wanted to go.

He put the phone on the table and went to the closed bathroom door and knocked. He opened it a crack.

"Dad, Tim's on the phone. Can I go to the shore with him and his family tomorrow?"

Steam billowed out the door, and Dad's muffled voice said, "Sure."

Doug closed the door and asked no one in particular, "How can he use hot water like that for a shower in the summer?"

I felt more hopeful. If Doug was going to spend tomorrow with Tim, maybe he'd spend other days with him, too. Maybe he would never spend another day with that terrible guy. Maybe I was worrying about nothing. Maybe I wouldn't have to say anything to anybody.

Maybe.

EAST EDGE
8
MYSTERIES

I finally fell asleep thinking about Harmony Hill, and I woke up Thursday morning feeling crabby and sad. What would I do with myself when everyone was at camp?

I didn't trust myself to be pleasant until almost ten o'clock. By that time, Shannon, Alysha, and I had already taken lots of books off the high shelves in Mrs. Bealer's bedroom and stashed them in boxes in the corner.

A big fan sat in the window blowing the hot air around. It wasn't any cooler than yesterday, but at least the air was moving.

The fan was Shannon's. Mom and Dad had no idea where ours was. I would be so glad to get back to Hampton Street.

At ten-thirty, Mrs. Wells came down from upstairs, and we had our tea party. Today a lemony fragrance floated up on the steam, and Mrs. Wells brought little sticky buns to nibble on. They were delicious, even if three bites were all you got out of each one.

I felt funny around Mrs. Wells. I wasn't used to adults getting mad at me, and I wasn't sure how to act. But I seemed to be the only one who remembered her sharpness with me. Mrs. Bealer was her sweet self, making Shannon feel welcome. Alysha was her usual chattery self, and Mrs. Wells seemed to be especially nice to me. I decided it was her way of apologizing.

"Do you do this every day?" I asked, hoping no crumbs were caught in the corner of my mouth.

"It takes the loneliness out of the day," said Mrs. Wells, passing the sticky buns as she talked. "Living by oneself is not fun. That's why I'll miss Emily so much. Who will I have tea with?"

"You'll just have to come to Maple Shade every day." Mrs. Bealer was wearing a bright blue sweater today, and it was buttoned to the neck. Just looking at her made me sweat.

"How about once a week?" Mrs. Wells asked.

"Really?" Mrs. Bealer's face lit up at the

thought. "You'd come see me that often?"

"Of course. You've been one of my closest friends since I moved here."

"How long have you lived in East Edge?" I asked.

"About five years. And Emily was the first person I met. She brought me a loaf of banana bread and invited me for tea. We've been getting together every day since."

"I can't tell you how nice it is to have someone over thirty living in this building." Mrs. Bealer reached for another sticky bun. "It's not that the young people aren't nice. It's just that they never have time to talk."

I did some rapid math and figured I could have one and three-fifths more sticky buns. The three-fifths would be a bit tricky.

"The people who last had your apartment, Myra, were about eighteen, if not younger. I don't think the young man even shaved yet. That was when I first thought about putting my name on the waiting list at Maple Shade. Now I've a wonderful neighbor, but my health is going. God always oversees the timing of these things, doesn't He?"

It was interesting to hear how naturally Mrs. Bealer referred to God. It was obvious that He and she were good friends.

"Are movers coming to take your things to Maple Shade?" asked Shannon as she sipped her tea.

Mrs. Bealer shook her head. "No movers. My son is driving up from New Jersey, and my daughter is coming from Scranton with her husband and three sons. They're going to be my movers."

"And they don't charge a penny for their labor," said Mrs. Wells with her warm smile.

Mrs. Bealer nodded. "And afterwards they'll even take me out to dinner anywhere I want to go. Regular movers won't do that."

We all laughed.

"See that picture?" Mrs. Bealer pointed to a silver frame that held a group of six smiling faces. "That's my daughter, Bonnie, and her family. Sara, my granddaughter, won't be coming because she has a summer job that requires her to work weekends. And that's Buddy, my son." She pointed to a smiling man. "He's a bachelor, but I think he's finally got a girlfriend. I hope he brings her."

It seemed kind of funny for a bald man like Buddy to have a girlfriend.

"Do you just have the two children?" asked Alysha.

Mrs. Bealer nodded. "They are my great joy,"

she said, quietly but proudly. "As are my grandchildren."

"Grandmom Jackson always says that about us,
too," Alysha said. She sat up straight, tilted her head,
and said in a slow, thick voice, "You are my pride
and joy, children. You are my pride and joy." Then
she collapsed into being herself, legs swinging,
teacup swaying as she rested it in her lap.

"I have a son who has been a source of pride,
too," said Mrs. Wells. "His name is David, and he's
a math professor in Atlanta, Georgia. I tell him
that there are only two things about him that I
don't like. One is that he lives so far away. The
other is that he never writes. He says math
professors aren't allowed to write. It's in their
contracts. I say piffle."

"Piffle!" Alysha bounced as though her chair
were a trampoline. "You said piffle!"

Mrs. Wells looked somewhat surprised by
Alysha's reaction.

"I never heard anybody but Grandpa Jackson
and me say it before!"

"Alysha says it all the time," I explained. "She
claims it's her family's word."

"But I don't mind sharing," she said quickly.
"You can say it, too."

"Thank you," said Mrs. Wells very seriously, but her eyes were sparkling with laughter.

We cleaned up the tea things for Mrs. Bealer and Mrs. Wells and went back to the bedroom.

"Oh, Cammi," Mrs. Bealer called.

I came into the living room and she handed me some money.

"You girls are very nice about drinking tea with us old ladies," she said, her feet up on the hassock. Her ankles looked really swollen. "But I know you prefer sodas. Run to the store and get two six-packs of whatever you girls would enjoy most."

I zipped out the door, thinking how cool the air conditioned food store would be. As I crossed the landing, I noticed for the first time that there was a staircase that led down to the back of the house. It was tucked out of the way and in the shadows.

I didn't think anyone would mind, so I tiptoed down to see where it ended. It was dim and narrow back there, not open and light like the front stairs. Maybe when the house was first built, before it became stores and apartments, the servants used this back staircase to run errands or do whatever servants did.

I imagined running up and down these steps in long skirts and aprons, arms full of laundry or a tray of food. It must have been so hot!

I pushed open the door at the foot of the stairs and found myself behind the building in the parking lot. Spaces for several cars were marked with yellow lines, though most of them were empty—probably because people were at work. One of the cars had a sticker on the back window for Georgia Tech. I figured that was Mrs. Wells's car. The other spaces probably belonged to the two young families that lived in the back apartments.

I turned to go back into the building, but the door wouldn't open. It had slipped shut behind me, and now it was locked. I shrugged and walked to the store down the alley.

I lingered as long as I could in the store, enjoying the air conditioning. I was glad to get in line behind a grouchy looking man who had a fairly large order. I could have stood behind a young mother with two crying kids and two carts of groceries, but I wasn't that hot.

"I have to carry all this," the grouchy man told the boy who was bagging. "Divide everything in half and double bag it, a paper bag inside a plastic one. And hurry up!"

When the grump left the store, I was glad it was he carrying all that stuff, not me.

The heat hit me in the face when the store door slid open. Maybe I should have picked the mom and the crying kids after all.

I gripped my sodas and walked with my head down, wishing I had a pair of sunglasses. I had to look up at the traffic light, and I saw the grouchy man with the two bags walking just ahead of me.

While I waited for the red light to change, I kept watching him. There wasn't anything else to look at. I was surprised to see him walk into Mrs. Bealer's apartment building.

He must live in one of the back apartments, I thought as I followed him to and through the door. But if he does, Mrs. Bealer's and my ideas of young are certainly different. This guy was more like the age of my father.

When I reached the landing near Mrs. Bealer's door, the man was on the third-floor landing. He set his bags down as he paused to catch his breath. For some reason, I stepped into the dimness of the back stairwell. I didn't know why, but I didn't want him to see me. He made me uncomfortable.

He took a few deep breaths, picked up his groceries, and went right to Mrs. Wells's door. I heard him rattle the knob, but of course the door was locked. Mrs. Wells always kept her apartment locked. The man made an angry sound and began to pound on the door.

Almost immediately it opened.

"Where have you been?" Mrs. Wells hissed, her voice angry. She didn't sound at all like the pleasant person we had talked with at tea just a few minutes before. In fact, she sounded like the person who had yelled at me yesterday, only angrier—a lot angrier. "Are you crazy, going out like that? What if somebody sees you?"

"Shut up!" the man said. I'd never heard such a nasty tone of voice, not even on TV. "I don't need you telling me what to do and what not to do! If I want to go out, I'll go out. So just butt out and shut up! Nobody saw me!"

The door slammed, the noise echoing in the empty lobby.

I walked into Mrs. Bealer's wondering about Mrs. Wells. Who was she really? Where had she come from? Was she a nice person or a nasty one?

One thing was for sure, though.

Mrs. Wells didn't live alone.

Dad went to the house on Hampton Street that evening, and Hal and I went with him. The house looked like it did before the fire, only fresher because of the new roof and the paint job.

The garage, where the fire had started, was all rebuilt, and the living room ceiling was fixed and the new rug laid.

I smiled. It wouldn't be long before we were back where we belonged.

I walked into my bedroom, which fortunately the fire had not reached, and it looked almost like it used to. Because of the soot and the smell, I had had to get a new rug, a new bedspread, and new wallpaper, but I got the same color, a pretty rosy pink that Dad said made me look pretty. I don't know what Brooke would have said, and I didn't plan to ask.

"Yo, Cammi!" It was Dee and Bethany at the front door. Dee lives across the street and down two houses. Bethany lives around the corner.

"How's Beast?" I asked.

We went and got him at Dee's house. He was so glad to see me that I started to cry. He made me laugh by licking my tears away.

I visited my doll collection, too, lined up along the floor in Dee's room. They let me know that while Dee was kind to them, they missed me and wanted to go home.

"Soon," I told them when Dee and Bethany weren't looking. I knew they didn't understand how I felt about my dolls. "Soon."

We took Beast with us back to my house, and he kept running in circles all around the yard, barking like crazy. He wanted to be home, too.

"Hal said he thought he saw Bugs in the woods yesterday," I told the girls. "Let's go look for him."

It wasn't hard to find where Hal had seen Bugs because he and the Denning twins were there, busy building their fort, which looked just like a dirt hole to me.

"I think it must have been him," Hal said,

"because some of the cat food I put out is gone."

"Bugs," I called. "Bugs! Where are you? Come here, boy! Come to Cammi."

The girls and I walked all around the woods, looking in any spot we thought a cat might hide. We didn't find him.

"Why hasn't he come home?" asked Bethany, sounding worried. Her little brother was very allergic to almost everything, so she had no pets except some fish. I think she looked at my pets as hers. "Was he hurt in the fire?"

"We don't think so," I said. "We think he was terrified and ran away out of fear. We were afraid he got himself lost or some animal got him. But maybe not." Happiness surged through me. "Maybe not."

We walked back to the house and there was Beast, worn out from all his circles, lying under the sycamore.

"Hey, big guy, come here!"

He looked at me and smiled, his tongue hanging almost to the ground, but he didn't move.

"Come here, Beast!" I clapped my hands.

He thumped his tail, but the rest of him didn't move.

I walked over to make sure he was all right.

Beast always came when you called, no matter where he was or how tired he was.

Suddenly I screamed, scaring even myself. Dad came running, and so did the girls, but Beast still didn't budge.

I ran and fell on my knees, wrapping my arms around the dog and the reason he wouldn't move. Sound asleep between Beast's front paws was Bugs, his gray coat blending with Beast's black one so that I hadn't seen him until I was very close.

My scream woke the cat, and he blinked his beautiful green eyes at me sleepily. He was very skinny, but he was purring, and he kept it up all night. I know because Dad helped Hal and me sneak him into our apartment, and he slept in my bed.

"If they evict us, so what?" Dad said. "We're moving out next week anyway."

Thank You, God. Bugs tonight and home next week!

When Doug finally got home from the shore, he was as delighted to see Bugs as the rest of us. Even Mom came into the bedroom to greet the cat when she got home from work.

"Sorry to wake you," she said, "but I had to see this furry guy." When she tickled him under the chin, his purrs rattled the windows.

It was hard for me to leave Bugs on Friday to go
to Mrs. Bealer's, but I didn't have any choice. There
was still work to be done. Dad dropped Alysha and
me off as usual.

"My mom's coming to get us around two this
afternoon," Alysha said. "I know that's early, but
Dad's getting out of work early because we're
going away for the weekend."

"That's fine," Dad said. "Doug will be at home,
so Cammi won't be alone."

We spent the first part of our day wrapping up
the china ladies. They were very beautiful, and I
was scared I'd chip or break one.

"How much do these things cost?" Alysha
asked as she wrapped up a pretty blond in a pink
gown and a big straw hat decorated with pink
flowers and ribbons.

Sometimes I admired her ability to ask questions.
Other times I was embarrassed. This time I almost
died. Mom always said it was very poor manners to
ask how much anything cost.

Mrs. Bealer didn't seem to mind. "The one you
are holding, Alysha, now costs about $125."

Alysha's eyes got huge, and I felt my fingers

become totally paralyzed.

A hundred and twenty-five dollars! If I broke one, I wouldn't have an allowance until I was twenty! I couldn't wait till the ladies were all packed and we could move on to the kitchen.

Mrs. Wells came down for tea just after we finished the ladies, bringing homemade lemon bread. If this job lasted much longer, I'd have a daily tea habit as strong as Mrs. Bealer's and Mrs. Wells's—which would present quite a problem when school started.

Today's tea was cinnamon, and I liked it the best of them all. It went very well with the lemon bread, and for once there was enough to eat to satisfy my hunger.

"Tell us about your families, girls," Mrs. Bealer said. "How about you, Alysha?"

"I have two brothers—Damon, who is seven and Thetis, who is four. As far as brothers go, they're okay, but they never sit still for a minute. They run and jump and hop all over the place. They especially like to practice tumbling off cliffs using the back of the sofa. They drive my parents and me crazy."

The ladies and I looked at Alysha in amazement. Her legs were twitching like she was pedaling a bike at top speed, and she was squirming in her seat. She must have stirred her tea at least fifty times, probably more like a hundred. Talk about not sitting still!

"Are they in gymnastics like you?" I asked.

"Damon isn't, but Thetis wants to start in the fall. I don't know if he'll be as good as me, but he'll be good. All that energy, you know."

We nodded. We knew.

"And what about you, Cammi?" Mrs. Bealer's sweater today was neon yellow with big gold buttons. Every single button was fastened, and she had a shawl over her legs.

"I have an older brother, Doug, and a younger brother, Hal. They're real good brothers, and I like them a lot. Hal was the one who found my cat for me." I told them the tale of Bugs.

All the time Alysha and I were talking about ourselves, I was trying to figure out how to ask about the man in Mrs. Wells's apartment, but without asking directly, if you know what I mean.

So I said, "You have two children coming to help you tomorrow, Mrs. Bealer. Do you have any more children, maybe some who live too far away to help?"

She shook her head. "Just Buddy and Bonnie."

"How about you, Mrs. Wells? Just the college professor?"

"David would be enough to make any mother proud," she said.

"So there are no more kids?"

"Any child the age of mine would hardly be called a kid," she said.

She was very good at not answering my questions.

Both the women were sad because this was their last tea time. They sat and talked long after Alysha and I had gone back to work.

We were in the kitchen, emptying all the shelves, when we heard a great crash over our heads. Alysha and I looked at each other, then at the ceiling.

"Mrs. Wells," I called. "Something or someone just fell in your apartment."

"Nonsense," she said. "There's nothing up there to fall."

"Well, there was just a great crash right over our heads."

She looked upset. "What could it possibly be? I'm all alone up there." She left quickly.

"Mrs. Bealer," I asked, "has Mrs. Wells always lived alone?"

Mrs. Bealer nodded. "I think her husband's dead, and of course her son lives in Atlanta. I met him once when he came to visit her. He seems a very pleasant man. I must say he doesn't look like a professor. More like an aging football player—all shoulders and muscles, but lots of gray hair."

I thought of the man I had seen yesterday. He was certainly no athlete. He couldn't even make it up two flights of stairs without having to rest. And his hair was more gone than gray.

Mrs. Bealer continued, "Once when we were talking about when our children were young, she accidentally let it slip that she had a second son. But she has never purposely told me anything about him. I don't know if he's dead, or whether he left home and never returned, or what."

I went back to the kitchen and the pots and pans.

"There's somebody up there with her, Alysha," I said. "I saw a man go into her apartment when I came back from the store yesterday. I don't understand why she keeps saying she's alone if there's someone up there."

"Maybe it's her boyfriend," Alysha said. "Maybe Buddy Bealer isn't the only older person to be in love."

"They're not in love," I said. "They hate each other. You should have heard them!"

At two o'clock, when Alysha had to leave, we weren't quite finished. I gave Dad a call at school.

"Can I stay a bit longer?"

"If you stay, I won't be able to get you until almost ten because of a dinner meeting I have to go to."

I decided to stay. I wanted everything to be done when Mrs. Bealer's family came tomorrow.

At six o'clock Mrs. Bealer announced that we should get a pizza down the street at John's.

"Get a large one, half plain and half pepperoni," she said. "Whatever we don't eat, my grandchildren will eat tomorrow."

I called ahead, waited fifteen minutes like they told me to, then walked down the street. The stores were all closed, but Denny's Deli, John's, and a Chinese restaurant were open. There was a slight breeze, and it felt good. I pushed John's door open and went in. Our pizza was waiting for me on the top of one of the ovens. It smelled wonderful.

I was trying to figure out how to open the store door with my hands full of our very large, very hot pizza when the door suddenly swung outward and

I found myself nose to nose with Doug. Behind him was the thief kid, and behind him, sleeves rolled up to the shoulder, was the big kid.

Doug and I just stared at each other. I'm not sure which of us was more surprised.

"Yo, Reston, move it," said the thief kid. "Let the girl out so we can get in."

"Unless, kid, you want to give us your pizza, huh?" It was the big guy, bending down and snarling in my face.

"Let her alone, King," Doug said.

"Protector of babies, huh, Reston?" King sneered.

I threw a panicky glance at Doug and ran. I didn't stop until I was inside Mrs. Bealer's building. My heart was pounding, and I was very scared.

Oh, God, I prayed, leaning against the hall wall, *Doug's with those guys again! What should I do? Tell, right?*

I climbed the stairs on shaking legs, then made

myself stand still. I couldn't rush into Mrs. Bealer's like this; I'd scare her to death. I took several deep breaths and felt my heart slow to normal.

Even so, Mrs. Bealer took one look at me and asked, "What's wrong, Cammi?"

For some reason I couldn't tell her about Doug. I wanted to protect him and his reputation.

"Some big guy scared me," I said, hoping that telling only part of my scare wasn't lying. "He threatened to take my pizza."

Mrs. Bealer clicked her tongue in distress. "I never thought you'd have trouble in the daylight!"

"Don't worry," I said. "I'm fine, and so's the pizza."

We ate in the living room on TV trays so she wouldn't have to walk. Then we watched "Jeopardy," and Mrs. Bealer got almost every answer, including the big one at the end. I was very impressed.

"Trivia," she said. "I'm good with trivia. I'm looking forward to lots of Trivial Pursuit games at Maple Shade."

From nine o'clock on, I kept checking out the window for my father's car. He was going to pull up right in front, and I didn't want to keep him waiting.

It was dark now, the street lights making pools of light that lessened into areas of dimness before the next pool began. The neon from Denny's Deli was reflected in the windows of cars parked along the curb, giving things a spooky red appearance.

"You know, downtown looks kind of pretty at night," I said. "Everything looks neater and cleaner."

There were a few people walking along the street and several groups, mostly young, lounging against buildings, talking.

Occasionally someone would laugh loudly or yell. It was weird to watch these shadowy people talking with their hands and slapping each other on the back and pointing to something I couldn't see.

A convertible drove by, top down, music blaring. The people inside shouted to everyone on the sidewalk, and everyone shouted back.

"It's like a party going on out there," I said.

"I've noticed it before," Mrs. Bealer said. "I think it's because it's Friday and the whole weekend's ahead."

I nodded. "I feel that way every Friday about three in the afternoon during the school year."

It wasn't difficult to recognize the big guy Doug had called King as a member of one lounging group. His size marked him easily.

As I stared at him, he slapped his arm a couple of times and then jerked his thumb towards Denny's Deli. The whole group turned as one and headed off.

I felt glad that something, in this case probably mosquitoes, could make King move against his will.

As King and his group filed into Denny's, the light from the deli shone on them. I wasn't surprised to identify either the thief kid or my brother.

I sighed deeply.

Oh, Doug, what are you doing?

Tears blurred my vision. I blinked and blinked, my back to Mrs. Bealer, until finally I could see normally again.

Another group came to lounge where Doug and King and the thief guy had been. I watched them as they talked and gesticulated. Were they telling jokes? talking about the Phillies? Were they old or young? Did any of them have a sister who would tattle on them?

When a car went by and bathed the group in its headlights, I was surprised to see that one of the new group was Mr. Ryan, a cop friend of my mom's. What was he doing loitering in downtown East Edge after dark?

The door to Denny's opened, and several young guys burst into the street. They each carried a small brown bag. Each bag contained a bottle—I could tell by the shape of the bags—and one guy was swigging from his bag as he walked.

Somehow I didn't think the bottles were full of Pepsi.

A sudden thought struck me with all the force of a baseball bat on a home-run ball. I sat up straight and stared first at Mr. Ryan and the people he was with. Then I looked at the guys with the bottles. Then I stared at Denny's.

A raid! The police were going to raid Denny's for underage drinking! And Doug was in there!

"Mrs. Bealer, I'll be back in a minute!"

I was halfway down the front stairs when I decided I should try to keep out of Mr. Ryan's way. He might try to stop me from going into the store.

I turned around and ran down the backstairs and out into the parking lot. It was dark and scary, and I didn't like the way I got goose bumps and heart palpitations. But the door had shut behind me, and I couldn't get back in the building. I was committed to warning Doug.

I made a large loop, running down the back alley to the side street, along that street and across

Lincoln Highway, on until I came to the alley behind Denny's.

Most of the stores and buildings had signs over their back doors to identify them, a convenience for both delivery men and customers who parked in the alley.

I found the sign that said Denny's Deli and grabbed the door knob. I had never been more scared in my life, not even the night of the fire.

I flew down the back hall past the rest rooms and burst into the deli-restaurant. My sudden and unexpected entrance stopped all conversation, and everyone turned to stare at me.

I was only half aware of the stares, though. I was looking for Doug.

He was standing with the thief guy and King at a large video game machine. His face was full of disbelief.

I ran straight to him. I had to get him out of there.

"Doug," I cried. "You've got to come. There's going to be trouble!"

Doug didn't move. I grabbed his arm and pulled. "Come on! Come on!"

"Hey," said King, staring at me through squinted eyes, "it's the little kid with the pizza. Get lost, kid.

We're busy. The only trouble around here will be yours if you don't get out."

There was no mistaking the threat in his voice.

"Doug! Come on! Mr. Ryan's outside!"

"Who is this girl?" asked the thief kid. "How does she know you?"

Doug shook his head like Beast does after a swim—I guess to throw off his confusion.

"She's my sister," he said. "Good-bye, Cammi."

"Doug, you don't understand! You've got to come with me!"

"Cammi, you don't understand. I'm not going anywhere."

"What?" I couldn't believe what I was hearing.

"I'm not going anywhere," he repeated. "I'm playing a game with some friends, and I intend to finish it and play several more. I'll leave when I want to and not before. And right now I don't want to."

I stared at him. It had never occurred to me that he wouldn't come with me. That he might even get mad at me.

"Doug! Please! Think what Mom and Dad will say!"

"And how will Mom and Dad ever find out?" he asked, looking at me through slitted eyes.

He scared me. He had never looked at me like that before, and I shivered.

Tattletale, ginger ale,
Stick your head in the garbage pail.
Turn it in, turn it out,
Turn it into sauerkraut.

"I'll have to tell," I whispered. "I'll have to because I love you."

The thief guy took me by the arm and spun me around, pointing me towards the front exit.

"Out, kid!" he said. "Now!"

He grabbed me by one arm and King took my other, and they walked me none too gently to the door. I twisted and looked back at Doug. He was standing by the game, staring at nothing, his face blank. When he realized I was watching him, he reached out for a bottle of Coke on the table next to the machine and took a long, casual swallow.

The message was clear. He didn't care about me or Mom or Dad or any standards we had been taught. He only cared about these new and terrible friends.

King and the thief guy all but threw me out the door.

"And don't come back," the thief guy called after me.

No problem there. I ran across the street and into Mrs. Bealer's building. Tears were streaming down my cheeks, and I felt all cold and shriveled inside.

Doug, my brother, my hero, had rejected me!

EAST EDGE 11 MYSTERIES

I tripped up the front stairs, blinded by my tears. I fell on the top step and lay there, sobbing.

The front door flew open, and I spun around with hope. Surely it was Doug, regretting what he had said.

It was Mr. Ryan. He was wearing jeans and a T-shirt, and he didn't look like a cop.

"Cammi! What are you doing here?" He looked worried and angry.

"I've been working for a lady who lives here."

"Who?" His voice was sharp.

"Mrs. Bealer. She lives right there." I pointed to her door.

"What were you doing at Denny's? That's not a safe place for a kid like you."

I shook my head. "I can't tell you."

"I can find out easily enough, you know."

I still shook my head. "I can't tell."

He either didn't have the time or the patience to argue with me.

"Well, you've got to get out of this hallway, and so do I. It's not safe here, either. Go into the apartment and stay there!"

"Yes, sir." I stood and turned, feeling tired and defeated.

"Good girl," Mr. Ryan said. He pulled the front door open. "Your mother would kill me if anything happened to you."

The door clicked shut behind him, and I sank back down on the top step. If Mrs. Bealer had been upset before when she saw how I looked, she'd be very upset now. I had to pull myself together before I could go in.

I wiped at my tears, trying to calm down, but I couldn't stop crying. I lowered my head to my knees and just sat.

Doug, Doug, Doug, what are you doing to us?

The footsteps on the stairs above me were soft, and I didn't really hear them until the man from Mrs. Wells's apartment joined me on the landing.

I looked up just as he saw me. He looked startled

and not very happy. Nobody seemed happy to see me tonight.

"Hi." I waved weakly and sniffed, making an awful noise. "Sorry. Did you hurt yourself when you fell this morning?"

"Er, hi," he answered. He hesitated. "Do you know me?"

"Sure," I said. "You're staying with Mrs. Wells. You're probably her missing son."

He looked at me sharply. "Did she tell you that?"

"No," I said. "I figured it out myself. You did something terrible and now you hardly ever see her."

I had a startling, upsetting thought and started to cry harder than before.

"Doug's going to turn out like you!" I wailed. "The cops are going to get him tonight, and he's going to have a runaway life, too!"

Mr. Wells, if that's who he was, narrowed his eyes at me.

"The cops are going to get *who* tonight?"

I sighed and sniffed again. "My brother. They're out front right now waiting to raid the place."

Mr. Wells jumped as though a snake had bitten him.

"The cops are here? Now?"

I nodded. "I just talked to one. Oh, what will Mom and Dad say? Especially Mom. She's a cop," I explained to the man.

"Your mother's a cop?"

I nodded. "And my brother's an almost criminal."

Mr. Wells took the gym bag he was carrying, balanced it on the bannister, and reached inside. I noticed for the first time that his one arm was wrapped in an elastic bandage.

"Did you hurt your arm when you fell this morning?"

"What makes you think I fell? And why do you think I'm Mrs. Wells's son?"

"I heard you fall this morning, and yesterday I saw you go into her apartment." I stood up, brushing off my seat. Something about the man suddenly made me uncomfortable. "I think I'll just go in now."

I edged my way toward Mrs. Bealer's door.

"Stay where you are, kid," he snarled as he pulled a gun out of his gym bag. Quicker than a lightning flash, he reached out and grabbed my wrist, jerking me close to him.

But he had grabbed me with his sore arm, and he winced with pain. I wriggled and turned as much as I could, hoping his arm would be too painful to hold me.

"Hold still or I'll knock you out," he hissed. The threat in his voice made me do just as he said.

Silently he wrapped his good arm around my waist and transferred the gun to his bad arm.

He pushed me toward the back staircase.

"The cops aren't here after you," I said. "You misunderstand. They're here to raid Denny's. Why would they want you?"

"I *know* the cops want me, kid. Escaped convicts are always wanted."

Escaped convicts!

"You first, kid." He pointed down the stairs. "But remember, the gun is faster than you could ever be, even in my bad hand."

I stumbled down the stairs, trying to think, trying to figure out how I could get out of this mess. But my mind was paralyzed. I was going through the mental equivalent of cardiac arrest.

"Flat line!" the nurse would yell. "No activity at all. Dead on her feet."

Think, I told myself. *Think!*

We came to the door at the bottom of the steps.

"Stand still, kid."

I did, and he turned out the stairwell light.

I made an involuntary cry as fear crashed over me like a hurricane wave.

"Shut up, kid. We're just getting our eyes used to darkness before we open the door."

I forced myself to be still and wait. I didn't want to do anything to make him angry.

"Okay," he said after a few long, long moments. "Push slowly and carefully, kid. And stay right in front of me. My gun is at your neck."

I shivered as I felt the muzzle, and, as I was told, opened the door onto a small concrete porch with a railing around it.

If six people squeezed together, they could all stand on the porch at the same time. A light shone immediately over the door with lots of insects buzzing around it. A small flight of steps led down to the parking lot.

While the parking lot had been almost empty the other day when I checked it, tonight it was crowded, and not just with the cars of the tenants. Three police cars were there, too, and the cops that went with them.

One of the cops was my mother.

"Cammi!" Her cry was soft and instinctive. Her eyes were wide with fear, and I knew I probably looked the same way.

Mr. Wells raised his gun to show it to everyone.

A large moth from the light over our heads dive-bombed us, scaring us both. I flinched and swatted as it buzzed my face, and Mr. Wells ducked.

There was a quick movement as one of the police—I'm not certain who—tried to take advantage of the distraction.

But Mr. Wells recovered much too quickly. He grabbed me by the shoulder and pulled me directly in front of him. Then he waved his gun and yelled, "Get back! Get back!"

God, I prayed. *Help!*

"All I want is safe passage," he said. "I don't want to hurt the girl, but I will if I have to. I want you to get all those police cars out of here. And you will all go in them."

The police officers all looked at each other, nodded, and began climbing into their cars, except for my mom. She started toward me. One of the men took her arm and pulled her back.

"Janie, no," he said. "Get in your car."

"I'm okay, Mom," I called. "I'm okay."

Of course I wasn't. I was weak with fear, and my shoulder burned where Mrs. Wells's son dug his fingers into me, holding me tightly.

Mom turned towards her car as though she were

113

in a trance. The man who had her arm opened the door, and she climbed in.

Mom, don't go! Don't leave me!

"You'll never get away," I said to Mr. Wells. I was proud of myself; my voice hardly shook.

The officer shut Mom in her squad car, and she stared out at me.

Mom, it'll be all right! It has to be, doesn't it? Just don't go! Don't leave me! God, help!

"That's enough! You're through!"

The voice was loud and strong and came, of all things, from *behind* Mr. Wells and me. I know I jumped with surprise, and so did he.

But my spirit soared. The cavalry was riding over the hill!

"I've got a gun in your back," barked the voice behind us. "Put your hands up."

Mr. Wells turned to see this new threat, and his gun moved from my neck.

"Eyes front!" yelled another, deeper voice behind us. "Just put your gun down and let the girl go!"

But the girl was already going. As soon as the gun moved, so did I. I threw myself sideways and grabbed for Mr. Wells's bad arm, knocking it against the metal railing as hard as I could.

Mr. Wells yelled and dropped his gun.

The police rushed the porch.

Mom grabbed me.

Mr. Ryan, coming out the back door of the apartment with a grinning Doug in tow, sputtered, "You Reston kids are driving me crazy!"

And Doug, my hero, grinned, holding his Coke bottle to Mom's back and saying again, but in a normal voice this time, "That's enough! Put your hands up."

We Restons sat in our backyard around our new picnic table. It was our first full day back in our house. We kept smiling at each other while Beast lazed peacefully under the sycamore, Bugs asleep beside him.

In fact, it was so great to be home Doug didn't even mind being grounded for two weeks.

When we had finally gotten home last Friday evening, he had confessed to Mom and Dad about his lies and stuff. I was so glad I didn't have to tell, but I knew I would have if things had ended differently. I loved him too much to let him make bad choices.

Now, sitting in the backyard, I leaned my head back and watched the clouds chase each other.

"Listen! I think I hear someone at the front door," Hal said. He ran around to check and came back right away.

"There are two ladies out front," he half-whispered. "One's really old and in a wheelchair."

I got up and hurried around front, Mom and Dad following.

In a few minutes we were all seated in the living room, and Mrs. Bealer was telling us about Maple Shade Village while her driver, a lady named Mrs. Franz, listened.

"In short," Mrs. Bealer concluded, "I think I'll be very happy there."

We all made encouraging noises, and I felt relieved. I had been worried that once she got there, she'd find she'd made a mistake and couldn't undo it.

"Now, Cammi," Mrs. Bealer said, "I have something for you. I know you appreciate my old books."

"I love them," I said.

Nodding, Mrs. Bealer held out a small package to me. I took it and pulled the paper off. Inside was another lovely old brown leather book with gilt letters and golden edged pages. *Little Women*, the title read.

"Thank you very much," I said, running my

hand gently over the letters. "It's beautiful!"

Mrs. Bealer straightened the collar of her dress over the red sweater she was wearing. "And now I want to meet Doug, your rescuer, and hear the story of Friday night."

I told the story of seeing Doug go into Denny's Deli with the guys I didn't like, and how I went to warn him that the police were coming.

"Of course, they weren't coming," I said. "They were there for Mrs. Wells's son, but I didn't know that."

"When the guys escorted Cammi to the door and almost threw her out, I felt like they had hit me," Doug said. "I was surprised at how upset I was. Then they came back to the video game we were playing and started mocking her. Then they mocked Mom and Dad."

"In the meantime," I said, "I was sitting on the top step outside your door, trying to stop crying so I could go in. That's when Mr. Wells showed up. Only his name isn't Wells, it's Wellman. Bruce Raymond Wellman. He was in prison for armed robbery when he escaped. He'd shot somebody in the robbery."

"Two somebodies," said Mom. "Neither died, but Bruce Wellman is considered dangerous."

"No wonder his poor mother didn't talk about him," said Mrs. Bealer.

Mom nodded. "She disappeared right after the trial, trying to forget, I guess. Her real name is Anna Myra Wellman."

"Mr. Wellman didn't hurt you, did he?" Mrs. Bealer asked.

I shook my head. "Not at all, but he sure scared me!"

Doug took up his story. "Back in Denny's, I was thinking fast about things. I was thinking of Mom and Dad and Cammi, and I was comparing them to King and Vince. I'd only been hanging around with those guys for a couple of weeks, but I already knew they were jerks. I guess I was trying to prove I was cool or something. You know, sometimes it's hard being both a principal's kid *and* a cop's kid."

"I would say you were very fortunate," said Mrs. Bealer.

"Thank you," said Dad. "I agree."

Doug grinned. "Me, too, now. Anyway, that night I was struggling. I kept picturing Cammi coming to save me, and I realized that I shouldn't be embarrassed about my family, but proud. So I took off after Cammi, to apologize and make sure she was all right."

"Mr. Wellman was escorting me down the back steps about then," I said. I wanted Mrs. Bealer to understand how the stories fit together.

"I got to the top of the front stairs just as Cammi opened the back door. The light suddenly shining up the dark staircase caught my eye. I looked down and saw this guy with a gun on my sister. So I tiptoed down the steps and stuck my Coke bottle into his back and told him to give up."

Mrs. Bealer shook her head in amazement. "You were very brave to do that, Doug."

Doug disagreed. "I was angry, I think. Angry at myself for being so dumb, and angry at that guy for hurting my sister."

I looked at Mrs. Bealer. "I think he was brave, too."

Doug shook his head, embarrassed. "When I ran across the street and into your building, a cop named Mr. Ryan saw me and came after me."

"He'd already chased and lectured me," I said.

"He was afraid I was going to mess up Wellman's arrest. He got to the first floor landing just in time to look down the backstairs and see me stick my Coke bottle in the guy's back."

"You gave him heart failure, Doug," said Mom. "He's still reeling." Mom's voice became Mr.

121

Ryan's. " 'There he was, Janie, holding a Coke bottle to the guy's back! A Coke bottle, for Pete's sake! I almost fell down the stairs trying to save him.' "

Mrs. Bealer laughed, then asked, "What happened to Bruce Wellman?"

"He's been returned to prison," Mom said, "and his sentence will be lengthened."

"How did you know where he was?" asked Mrs. Bealer's driver. She had gotten as involved with the story as Mrs. Bealer.

"His mother called us. She was becoming scared for her own safety because of his fierce temper."

"Poor Myra," said Mrs. Bealer. "What emotional pain she must live with."

We were all quiet for a minute.

Then Mrs. Bealer asked, "Well, Cammi, what will you do with the rest of your summer?"

I shook my head. "Nothing special." My heart still shriveled whenever I thought of Harmony Hill. It was funny how I could be so happy about being home one minute and so sad the next.

"What do you mean, nothing special?" said Mom. "You leave Saturday for Harmony Hill."

I looked at her, confused, then I shook my

head. "Not this year, remember? We can't afford it because of the fire."

Now Mom looked confused.

"You said to Dad that Harmony Hill went up in smoke," I said. "I heard you."

Mom looked at Dad, but he only shrugged.

"You and Dad were talking about what you lost in the fire," I said. "And you said you guessed Harmony Hill went up in smoke, too."

Mom thought for a minute, then she blinked and sat up straight. "The mail!" she said. "The check to Harmony Hill was in a pile of mail on the seat of the car, waiting to go out the next morning. Harmony Hill and all the rest went up in smoke when the car and garage went. But, Cammi, I just sent another check a couple days later. You're all set to go."

"I am?"

Mom nodded. "All set."

My shriveled heart was suddenly full and bursting with joy, and I couldn't stop grinning.

Be sure to read about Shannon's week at camp in
East Edge #3 *Mystery at Harmony Hill*.

I had almost fallen asleep when I heard her move quietly, getting a raincoat, a flashlight. I heard her open the door and go out into the rain.

I reached for my flashlight and leaned over the bed. I looked down and shone my light quickly. As I expected, there was an empty bunk.

I slid to the floor and reached for my sneakers. They were right where I'd left them. I rolled my pajama pants up above my knees and slipped my raincoat on. The material crackled so loudly in my ears that I expected everyone to sit up and tell me to shut up.

I tiptoed to the door and opened it quietly. I stood on the porch and looked around. It was dark and difficult to see in the rain even though the light at the edge of the field was on and the wash house was lit as usual.

I went down the steps, afraid I'd lost her already. The rain beating on my hood made it impossible to hear any sound but my own heartbeat. I stepped into a puddle and felt the water pour into my shoes. I thought longingly of my dry bed.

At that moment I saw her. She was over by the dining room, and she had turned her flashlight on for a second. She went around the corner of the building and out of sight.

She was going toward the creek. I hurried across the field and around the corner after her. At first I thought the wild roar that struck me was my own hammering heart, but I realized with surprise that it was rushing, turbulent water. French Creek was going crazy!